BIG TRUCKS

written by Mary Gribbin
illustrated by Julian Baker

Ladybird

Words in **bold** are explained

in the glossary.

Ladybird books are widely available, but in case of
difficulty may be ordered by post or telephone from:

Ladybird Books – Cash Sales Department
Littlegate Road Paignton Devon TQ3 3BE
Telephone 01803 554761

A catalogue record for this book is available
from the British Library

Published by Ladybird Books Ltd Loughborough Leicestershire UK
Ladybird Books Inc Auburn Maine 04210 USA

BIG TRUCKS

Contents

Dumper Truck

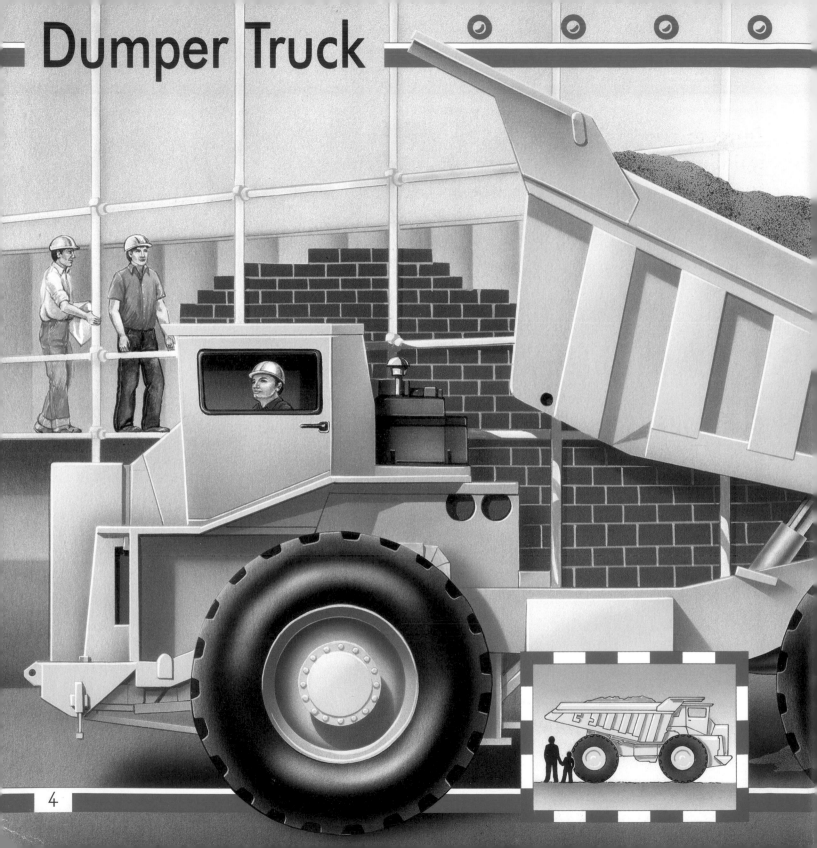

Dumper trucks deliver sand and gravel to building sites. Dumper trucks tilt from side to side as they go over the bumpy, uneven ground of building sites. The driver tips the sand and gravel out of the truck where the load is needed. The driver then lowers the body of the truck back to its base and drives off to the road.

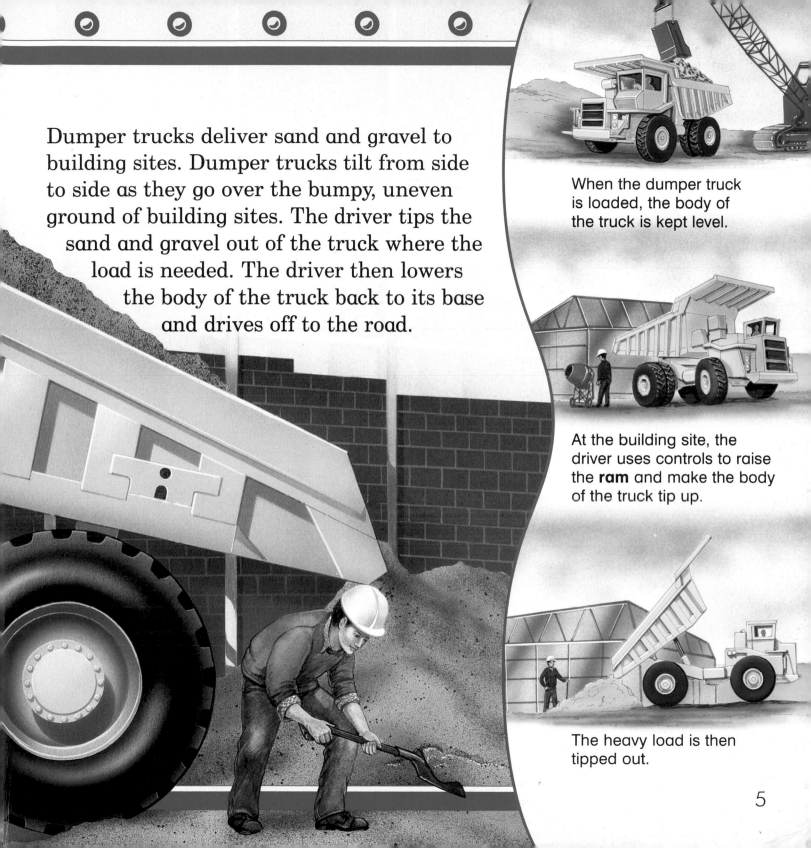

When the dumper truck is loaded, the body of the truck is kept level.

At the building site, the driver uses controls to raise the **ram** and make the body of the truck tip up.

The heavy load is then tipped out.

5

Road rollers are slow and heavy. They have huge metal rollers instead of tyres. The rollers are hollow, but they can be filled with water to make them heavier. Road rollers are used when new roads are made or when old roads are being repaired.

The paver spreads tar and small stones over the bumpy road surface.

The roller moves slowly over the **tarmac** to flatten it.

Once the tarmac is smooth and has hardened, cars and trucks can use the road. It will last for many years.

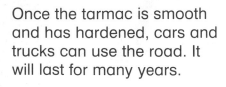

Snowplough

Snowploughs are used to clear heavy snow off the roads in winter. They have big tyres with large **treads** to stop them slipping and sliding on icy roads. Powerful headlights help the driver to see the road in bad weather or at night.

As the snowplough moves along, the metal faceplate on the front pushes the snow to the side and clears the road.

Grit is then scattered from the back of the snowplough onto the road. This makes the road safer and less slippery for cars.

Transporter Truck

Transporter trucks are used to take **goods** from one place to another. Large, wide wheels help to carry the weight of the load and make the truck safer to drive. The back or the side of the truck opens up for loading.

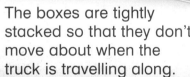

A forklift truck loads boxes into the back of the transporter truck.

The boxes are tightly stacked so that they don't move about when the truck is travelling along.

The boxes are unloaded and the delivery is made.

Sometimes the **cab** at the front of the truck has a bed, where the driver can rest after a long journey. The curved roof of the top of the cab makes it easier for the driver to steer the truck in windy weather.

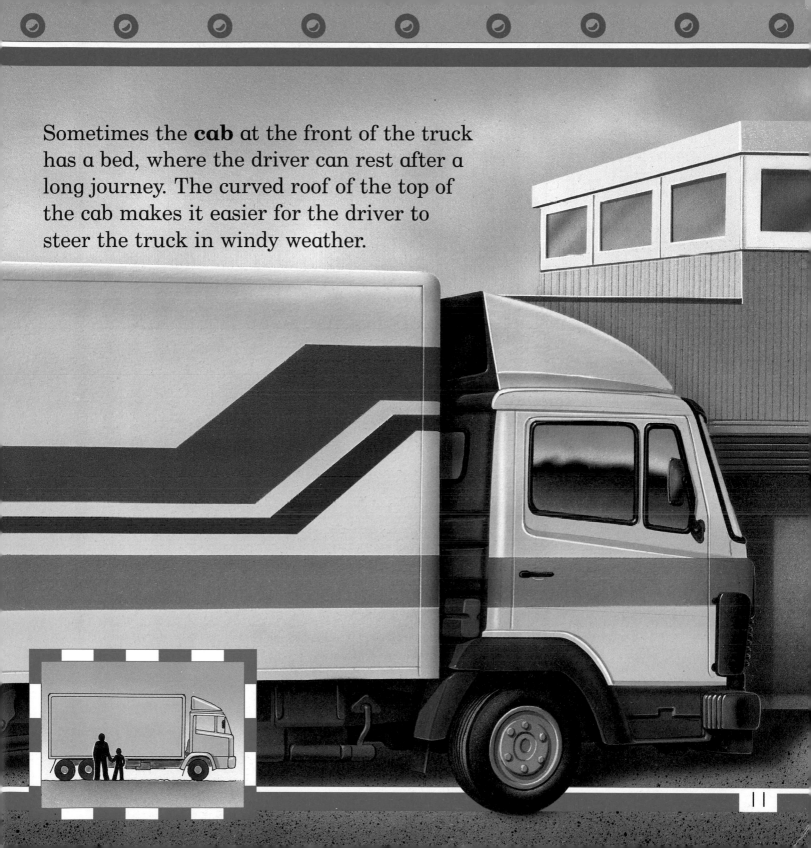

Tanker Truck

Tankers transport liquid **chemicals**, which are often dangerous. Tankers also transport some foods such as milk. The load is carried in a long, metal tank behind the cab.

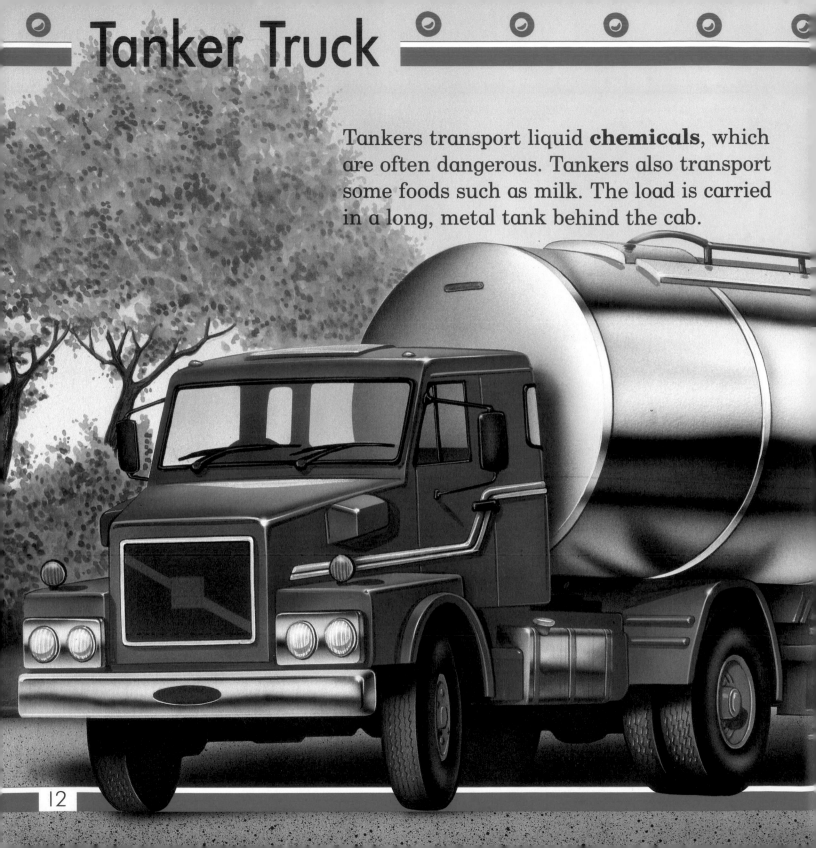

Large rear view mirrors on the side of the cab help the driver to see the traffic. When reversing, the truck makes a beeping sound to warn people to move out of the way.

A petrol tanker is filled with petrol at the refinery.

The tanker truck arrives at the petrol station.

At the petrol station, the petrol is emptied into tanks underneath the pumps.

Car Transporter

Car transporters collect new cars from the factory and take them to a car showroom to be sold. Most car transporters have more than one deck and can carry many cars at the same time.

A **ramp** is lowered and the new cars are driven up onto the top deck.

Then the bottom deck is filled. All the cars are tied to the **trailer** with strong cable to stop them from rolling off.

At the showroom, a driver carefully reverses the cars off the trailer.

Bigfoot Truck

Bigfoot trucks have enormous, tough wheels so that they can be driven over very rough ground or **obstacles**. Bigfoot trucks are driven for fun and for doing **stunts**. All bigfoot trucks have an especially strong frame that protects the driver if the truck crashes.

Tyres with thick treads stop the bigfoot from slipping and skidding.

The bigfoot can be driven on two wheels.

The driver wears a tight **safety belt** to prevent him or her from falling out.

17

Tractor

The plough makes **furrows** in the soil.

The spikes on the harrow break up the soil. Then seeds are planted in the furrows.

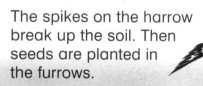

The crops are sprayed with fertilizer to help them grow.

Tractors are used on farms. Tractors have very large wheels and rubber tyres with deep treads. These help the tractor to drive over muddy, bumpy fields. Tractors can be used to work farm machinery. They pull ploughs and **harrows** to dig and break up the earth. Tractors also pull seed planters and fertilizer sprays. This helps the farmer to plant crops.

Combine Harvester

Combine harvesters are used to cut crops in the fields. Combine harvesters can cut huge fields very quickly. The driver sits in the cab, away from the dust and noise of the machinery. The grain from the crops is made into flour, bread and breakfast cereal.

The huge reel at the front of the combine harvester turns and cuts the crops.

An **elevator** carries the grain up into the threshing drum. Here, the grain is cut off the stalks and sent into a tank.

Then the grain is passed out of the combine harvester and collected in a trailer.

21

Fascinating Facts

Dumper Truck

Dumper trucks which carry heavy loads have extra wheels fitted to stop the trucks tipping over.

Road Roller

Old fashioned steam powered road rollers can be seen at special shows.

Snowplough

Some snowploughs can be fixed to the front of lorries and tractors.

Transporter Truck

Transporter trucks can travel on big boats to transport goods from one country to another.

Tanker Truck

Tankers carrying milk are refrigerated so that the milk is kept cool and fresh while it is being transported.

Car Transporter

Large car transporters can carry up to fourteen cars. The cab of the transporter may be separated from the car decks and driven on its own.

Bigfoot Truck

The frames of bigfoot trucks are just like the frames of ordinary vehicles, but they are raised off the ground by big wheels.

Tractor

The first tractor with a petrol engine was made in 1892, in America. Tractors replaced horses for pulling ploughs.

Combine Harvester

The combine harvester was invented by Hyram Moore in 1838, in America.

Glossary

Cab The front part of a truck where the driver sits.

Chemical A substance such as petrol, oil or paint.

Elevator A machine which lifts up boxes and other goods.

Furrow A deep, long hole in the ground made by a plough.

Goods Items which people need, and which can be moved on trucks, trains or ships.

Harrow A special machine with spikes that is pulled by a tractor. The spikes on the harrow break up and smooth lumps of soil.

Obstacle An object which obstructs or stands in the way.

Ram The rod which lifts up the body of the truck so that the load can be tipped out.

Ramp The sloping, back part of a transporter truck. Cars drive up the ramp when they are being loaded onto the truck.

Safety belt A harness which stops a person from being thrown forward in an accident.

Stunt An amazing and difficult act which people like to watch.

Tarmac The dark covering on roads. When tarmac is hot, it is sticky and it has a distinctive smell. Tarmac hardens as it becomes cool.

Trailer A vehicle that carries objects and which is pulled along by a car or lorry.

Tread The groove round the outside of a tyre. The tread helps a tyre to grip the road.

Index

Comparative sizes

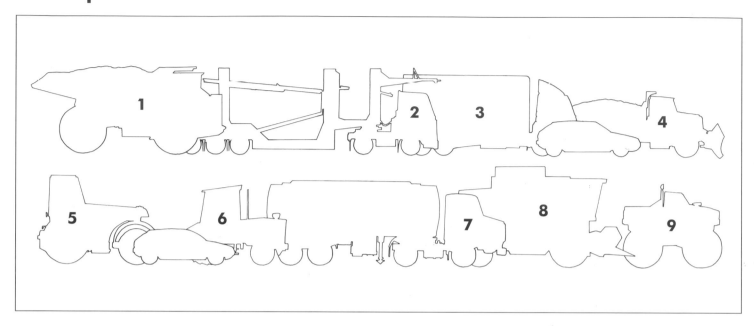

1 Dumper Truck

Some dumper trucks are so big that the driver has to use a ladder to climb into the cab.

2 Car Transporter

Some of the biggest car transporters can carry up to fourteen cars in a zigzag stack.

3 Transporter Truck

The biggest transporter truck carries the space shuttle to its launch pad. The truck moves so slowly that you could overtake it at a normal walking pace.

4 Snowplough

The biggest snowplough has a blade measuring fifteen metres, which is wider than a swimming pool. It was made in 1992 to clear the runway at an airport in New York, America.

5 Road Roller

A road roller can weigh as much as eighteen family cars.

6 Tractor

The wheels on some tractors are taller than a grown-up.

7 Tanker Truck

Tanker trucks can hold 36,000 litres of liquid. This is as much water as in 1,000 baths.

8 Combine Harvester

In one hour, combine harvesters cut enough wheat to equal the weight of four elephants.

9 Bigfoot Truck

The tracks made by the wheels of some of these trucks are wider than a small car.